To Shirl —
a wonderful friend
Carol

TAYLOR CREEK

by

Carolyn Nottingham

This is a work of fiction. Any resemblance of any of the characters to persons living or dead is strictly coincidental.

FIRST EDITION

Copyright 1997, by Carolyn Nottingham
Library of Congress Catalog Card No: 96-91037
ISBN: 1-56002-728-2

**UNIVERSITY EDITIONS, Inc.
59 Oak Lane, Spring Valley
Huntington, West Virginia 25704**

Cover by Linda Rzoska

Dedication

For my friend Marilyn

If the burdens of this life earn stars in heaven

you are destined for a celestial paradise

TABLE OF CONTENTS

CHAPTER 1
Marilyn Maier — 5
CHAPTER 2
John Westin — 10
CHAPTER 3
Christopher Dunn — 15
CHAPTER 4
John's Obsession — 17
CHAPTER 5
Marilyn's Awakening — 19
CHAPTER 6
The Picnic — 21
CHAPTER 7
The Storm — 23
CHAPTER 8
Marilyn & John — 28
CHAPTER 9
Conflict — 31
CHAPTER 10
Confrontation — 35
CHAPTER 11
The Agony — 40
CHAPTER 12
The Letter — 44
CHAPTER 13
Christy — 48
CHAPTER 14
Breakthrough — 52
CHAPTER 15
Full Circle — 56

CHAPTER 1
MARILYN MAIER

It was already 4:30 when Marilyn hurried into the supermarket. She needed a few ingredients for a casserole she was taking to a 6:00 p.m. reception at her church and due to a last minute detail at her job, she was running very late. As she got into line at the express checkout, she carefully avoided looking at the tabloids which were always displayed at the entrance of each checkout lane. However, when a customer in front of her caused a delay, she couldn't avoid the temptation to once again scan the headlines. There again, in bold print, **CHRISTOPHER DUNN'S SHOCKING AFFAIR WITH LIZA GILLIAN** was emblazoned across each tabloid. She was at once angry with herself. She knew that most of these stories were grossly untrue. Indeed, anyone that would report a two-headed baby fathered by a space alien left a lot to be desired in the credibility department. She wondered, though, if Christopher's marriage really was floundering. Unfortunately, the tabloids and magazine articles were her only link to Christopher.

She purchased her grocery items and hastily ran to her car, mentally sorting out her agenda for the evening. First she had to pick up her daughter Christy from her mother's, get the casserole prepared and in the oven, then go over the program for tonight's reception. She was a church organist, and in this capacity also took care of any extracurricular music at her church. Tonight's reception required a few sing-alongs and a duet sung by the Weber twins.

At a very early age Marilyn had displayed musical talent. She was only three when she charmed the entire congregation of her church by singing "Silent Night" at the Christmas Eve pageant. Throughout her youth she had taken piano, organ and voice lessons and just about always had the lead in every stage show, play, or musical. It was no wonder that soon after high school, instead of going on to college, she wanted to test her skills on the avenues of New York and Broadway. She was fresh, eager and ready. Her drama and music teachers encouraged her—they said she had talent and potential. Her parents finally supported her decision to go to New York. But a year later she returned home, broken hearted and pregnant, and, had broken her parents' heart as well.

Yes, she had hurt them. Nice girls in this community did not get pregnant without the benefit of matrimony. She knew what her parents endured—all the whispering and gossip when the news of her pregnancy became known. *No, Marilyn is not giving up the baby for adoption . . . she wants to keep it. No she won't tell us who the father is . . . only that he is married to someone else and she will not interfere in his life . . .* Her only reprieve was to focus on the fact that she was having a baby—her's and Christopher's. A child was all she would ever have of Christopher and no one could take that away from her.

She at last arrived at her parents' farm. The willows that graced the driveway brushed the top of her car as she drove in. It was always so beautiful here. A rolling farm in Michigan with woods across the way aglow with autumn glory. Her mother cared for Christy while she worked and she was grateful. She owed her parents so much for all she had put them through, but they had long since forgiven her. They loved their grand-daughter dearly and now would not have changed any circumstances surrounding her birth.

Marilyn worked at a hospital in nearby Hillsburg. She got the job soon after Christy was born. She began in billing and recently advanced to the Utilization Review Department. Today it was her new job that caused her to be running late and she needed to pick up her daughter and be on her way.

Five-year-old Christy was waiting for her and hopped into the car as her mother rushed out to make sure she did so.

"Are you going to get your dish for the reception ready in time?" her mother asked.

"Yes, it won't take long to prepare, but it needs to bake for thirty minutes so I must be going. By the way," Marilyn added, "have you met the new pastor yet?"

"No, not yet, but Aunt Bert said she met him and his family this morning. It's such a tragic story. He has two youngsters, 9 and 12, and his wife died of cancer. He took it very hard," mom added, with her usual display of anguish when a fellow Lutheran was suffering.

"It must be difficult for him . . . raising two kids without a mother."

"Well, he will certainly have a lot of motherly support from the women of our congregation, of that you can be sure." With that she blew Christy a kiss. "Bye-bye sweetie, see you tonight."

Marilyn was raised in a tightly-knit German-Lutheran community. Everyone knew everyone else's business, so the main topic of discussion lately was the arrival of the new minister at St. Luke's. They had been without a pastor for almost a year and during the vacancy had been served by a pastor from nearby Hillsburg. The congregation was now thrilled to finally have their own shepherd for their flock and were honoring him and his family this evening with a welcoming reception.

She drove the short distance to her home which was near to her parents' home on the other side of Taylor Woods. It was the old Liebermann farm. Many years ago her father had purchased the property—all except the house that Mr. Liebermann, a retired widower, lived in. Dad had worked the land now for more than twenty years. When old Mr. Liebermann died, his children had no interest in maintaining the home and decided to sell it. They approached her father, who already had access to all the outbuildings and asked if he would be interested in buying the house as well. He agreed.

Her father rented out the Liebermann house for a few years, but when she returned from New York it luckily lay vacant. After all the trauma of her situation was dealt with, she herself, suggested living there. It held a certain charm for her and it was also remotely tucked away on the north side of Taylor Woods. There was a trail behind the house leading down to Taylor Creek and it was quiet and peaceful there. Deer often congregated at the bottom of the hill by the creekside and it was a delight to watch them. She knew it was the perfect place to "lick her wounds," so to speak.

So during the remainder of her pregnancy she set to work to make the Liebermann home, her home. She did much of her own painting, wallpapering, sewing, and then, with just about the last of her savings and some additional help from her father, purchased a lot of rather nice antique furniture at garage and estate sales in the area. She liked the results. The home had an air of old-fashioned warmth with a touch of the unique, and most of all, she could afford it.

In spite of the bittersweet memories of her abandoned dreams, her life was stable and secure now. She was, however, still trying to sort out her feelings for Christopher and how she might have misinterpreted his feelings for her. She wondered if Christopher had ever attempted to get in touch with her. When she left New York she also left behind her other identity. Mary Mayer was a stage name she adopted and this was the only name Christopher knew her by.

Once again she tried to push these thoughts away. He certainly had plenty of opportunity to contact her if he had wanted to. She had waited for weeks, and when she discovered she was pregnant, she put her pride aside and called him, only to discover he was on his honeymoon. And then it was pride that would not allow her to inform Christopher of her pregnancy. Above all she did not want to become a "problem" in his life—she didn't want that role. At that point she realized she would have to return home to Michigan. She also thought it best not to divulge Christopher's identity to her family—her two older, overly protective, brothers might have brought him back to her at gunpoint!

She knew that at this time she needed to keep Christopher's identity a secret for a totally different reason. Christopher Dunn had become very well known. The media was constantly at his heels and he was second only to Princess Di in tabloid exploitation. She knew that if news leaked to the tabloids that Christopher had a child they would be hounded unmercifully and their lives would be forever changed.

She met Christopher at a cast party. She was thrilled when she learned that the actual creator of the production she was appearing in would be present. However, when she noticed a rather handsome redhead, with hair falling into his eyes, walk in, she was astonished to learn that *he* was Christopher Dunn. She didn't know what Christopher looked like, but she imagined a slightly more sophisticated, well tailored man. He was from London, after all, and apparently came from wealth.

That evening Christopher was dressed very casually in a loose fitting flannel shirt and khaki pants. He had wire rimmed glasses which mirrored his intelligent eyes, except that his hair kept getting in the way! They almost immediately struck up a conversation and their friendship began.

She realized that someday Christy would ask about her father and she supposed that Christy had a right to information regarding her parentage. She wanted Christy to know about her first impressions of Christopher. She first fell in love with his talent—he was a phenomenon of the musical theater. He was a genius. She was fortunate enough to have a part in his first success, *Night Train*.

She also wanted Christy to know her father was a man of integrity—that he was genuinely honest with her from the beginning. He in no way set out to conquer her. When he realized the relationship was becoming a bit more than just a friendship, he carefully explained to her that he was engaged and the wedding invitations were all but in the mail. He regretted that they had met too late and he did not want to hurt her.

After that conversation, she tried to avoid Christopher as much as possible. She did not trust herself in his presence and feared she would do or say something foolish. The night before Christopher was to fly back to London there was a farewell party given for him but she did not go. Instead she stayed home and tried to busy herself with personal projects, but there seemed no way she could ease the ache she felt in the pit of her stomach.

Later that evening her doorbell rang—It was Christopher. He said he could not leave without first saying good-bye. In an instant they were in each other's arms and were lost in the ecstasy that followed. She had no doubt in her mind that night that Christopher felt the same way about her as she felt about him. He left early the following morning to catch his flight. The last thing he said was, "I will work things out in London, Mary." Well, obviously he didn't work things out and life had to go on.

She still wondered if she had made the right decisions along the way. She once dated a man who had questioned her at length regarding Christy's father. She, of course, divulged nothing, but he made a comment that troubled her. He said that he believed Christy's father deserved to know he had fathered a child and since then she felt confused and uncertain.

As she left for the reception she wondered if perhaps the new minister, John Westin, might be someone she could someday confide in. She knew that he would perhaps offer wise counsel, but she was still reluctant to relate her story to anyone. She felt it liken to pulling a thread with the fear of having the whole garment unravel. This frightened her. More than anything she needed to protect her daughter.

CHAPTER 2
JOHN WESTIN

John marveled at his surroundings and again breathed a prayer of thanks. This indeed was God's garden. Perhaps here he could learn to live again—without Elizabeth. The past three years had been a hellish nightmare with the onset of Beth's illness and her subsequent death. His life seemed to unravel thread by thread after he heard the words, "ovarian cancer." Maybe now he could try to knit his life back into some pattern of sanity. He almost lost his faith, questioning how God could allow his wonderful wife to endure this illness and for their children to lose a most remarkable mother, but God's grace was ever present and he somehow got through those terrible dark days.

He met Beth while he was in the seminary. She was studying to be an elementary teacher. He loved her warm, outgoing personality—everyone was her friend—she had no enemies. She had beautiful brown eyes that attached their total attention to anyone she happened to be with. Beth was tall and slim (perhaps a little too slim for most men's standards), but he loved her energy and vitality. She made him happier than he had ever known he could be. They were married just shortly after he left the seminary.

He was then called to St. Mark's as an assistant pastor where there also happened to be a first grade position available at St. Mark's school, which Beth was accepted for. Life was good then, and three years later John became senior pastor. It was a large church and demanded much of him, but he led a prolific ministry and was diligent to his calling.

He and Elizabeth also produced two beautiful children, Michael and Bethany. Bethany, however, posed a difficult pregnancy for Elizabeth and she was bedridden for the last three months of her term due to toxemia. Because of this, John thought it advisable that he have a vasectomy since he did not want his wife to endure another pregnancy like the last one. Little did he know what else lay in store for Beth.

Throughout Elizabeth's illness there was much he left undone for the church, but the people of his congregation were very understanding. He felt badly, but he could not be all things to all people at that time. Then after Elizabeth's death, he threw himself back into his work, but much to the detriment of his children, as they needed him more than ever. He was also haunted by memories of Beth—everything reminded him of things they had done together, laughed about together, and dreamed about together. He wondered if he was going to make it through this after all. Finally, his bishop, Carl Keen, proposed something to him that he thought about very seriously.

"John," he said, "you need to leave this church and city and try to rebuild your life with your children. I really think you should take on a much smaller congregation, one that doesn't require so much of your time so that you can devote more of yourself to your kids. They don't have a mother now . . . it's just you. Remember that. There happens to be a small church in rural Michigan that has been waiting for a pastor for about a year now. I don't know if you would be interested or not, but I can call them and make a recommendation."

He was interested and now he was pastor of St. Luke's in Taylor Creek. The fresh air itself seemed to revitalize him and he already had gone horseback riding this morning. Bill Waggoner, from an adjacent farm welcomed him by offering to take Michael and Bethany riding first, and then offered John a chance to ride as well. Bill suggested they take a tour of the countryside.

They left the children in the capable hands of Bill's son, Kevin, and then he and Bill rode down to Taylor Creek and up through the path in the woods and then all the way down Taylor Creek Road. The trees were at the height of their October majesty and the sun seemed to form a halo above them with their brilliance. Everywhere they rode he marveled at the beauty of the countryside with hills and valleys ablaze with color reaching out to touch each horizon.

After riding, he and the children walked back to the parsonage. He could tell that the kids were having a wonderful time. They were not really certain that they wanted to move to a rural area, but this morning's adventure was beginning to shift their opinion.

The church, too, was picturesque. A small white-steepled building nestled in a grove of trees. The parsonage was next to the church. It was spotlessly clean (no doubt the women in the church had presented it so) and the refrigerator and cabinets were unbelievably stocked with food. These good people had made him feel most welcome. He again wished that Elizabeth could be here—*why couldn't they have shared this together?*

Tonight there would be a reception to further welcome him and he was looking forward to meeting these people and to thank them for their warm generosity. He had met with one of the church elders this morning who briefed him on things he should perhaps know in advance. To be forewarned is to be forearmed, as they say. He found out that Jennie Kruger had recently lost her husband in a freak farm accident; that Oliver Gerske's wife was seriously ill and in the hospital; and Mavis Jenkins would "not leave him alone."

"Best to just ignore Mavis," Elder Elmer Shiller warned.

Well, he'd have to play that one by ear, John thought.

"Another thing," Elder Shiller added, "the music gal, the one that plays the organ, Marilyn Maier, she has a little girl but she's not married . . . so don't go asking about her husband or anything."

And so much for the "scandal" in Taylor Creek, John mused.

Later in the morning a Mrs. Walter Maier paid him a visit with a warm cinnamon strudel in hand. The aroma was magnificent. They chatted for a while, and once again he was given a lot of details about the church, the people in the congregation, and the area in general. Mrs. Maier, or Bert, as she wished to be called, was an aunt to the organist, Marilyn, and she praised her niece's abilities extravagantly.

After spending the afternoon unpacking more boxes it finally came time for him and his family to make their way to the church for the reception. The reception was taking place in the church basement fellowship hall. Kevin Wagonner, who had taken the children horseback riding earlier that day, had already arrived. He left Kevin in charge of keeping the kids company as he needed to go upstairs to get some papers that he had left in his new office earlier.

When he arrived upstairs, he thought for a moment he was seeing double. There were identical twin girls sitting by the piano near the front of the sanctuary. They introduced themselves as Darla and Denise Weber. They explained they were singing a duet and were waiting for their accompanist. They were supposed to rehearse the music briefly upstairs as people were already beginning to congregate downstairs in the fellowship hall.

Just as he looked down at his watch to check the time, he heard a rushing sound behind him. As he turned around, he was absolutely astounded. There standing before him was the most astonishingly beautiful woman he had ever seen. She had amazing crystal blue eyes, long beautiful chestnut hair—and she had the smile of an angel.

"Hi," she said, "I'm Marilyn Maier, the church organist. You must be Pastor Westin. The clerical collar gave you away." She laughed as she extended her hand, "I'm so happy to meet you."

He hoped that he wasn't smiling at her stupidly with his mouth agape and quickly responded, "Yes, Ah . . . I've heard all about your marvelous musical abilities from your Aunt Bert this morning."

"Oh, she brags about me all the time. You'll have to make your own judgment, I'm afraid." Then she turned to address the twins. "I'm really very late . . . sorry girls . . . we'd better get to work." Then she turned back to him and said, "we probably shouldn't rehearse this in your presence as the twins are singing this in your honor later."

"Oh, of course," he stammered, "I . . . I need to pick up some papers from my office and then will be going downstairs. We'll need to talk later, though, I'd like to discuss the weekly order of service with you."

"Sure thing," she said. "I'll see you later then." She then again smiled that brilliant smile.

As he was returning to the fellowship hall he wondered at the incredible gene pool that evolved such a beautiful woman. She couldn't have been more than twenty-four or twenty-five, and she had such composure and self-assurance. Then he quickly admonished himself—what am I doing admiring beautiful young girls? Must be this *country air.*

When he found Michael and Bethany, they were surrounded by seven or eight other children about the same age. They seemed to have gained some instant popularity. He hoped that his decision to come to Taylor Creek would benefit them all. It was very important to him that his children be happy.

The reception was a beautiful affair with an abundance of delicious home-cooked food. The program was very nicely done and the twins sang beautifully. He also met Mavis Jenkins, and after about ten minutes of her machine-gun prattle, he thought he might better have heeded Elder Shiller's warning. Somehow he extricated himself from "Mavie" and made his way over to where Marilyn Maier was standing with a group of people. She introduced them, beginning with her little girl, Christy.

Christy began her introduction with, "I'm going on a bus every day to school, and I sit with Chad, and then I go to my granny's house, and then Mama comes and gets me, and then we . . ."

"And then," Marilyn interjected, "we need to give other people a chance to say something."

Everyone chuckled and Marilyn proceeded to introduce her family which were standing around her. There were her parents, Margaret and Edward; her brother Ed Jr. and his wife Joan and their daughter, Brandy; another brother Gary and his wife, Pat. Also nearby were her Aunt Bert, whom he had met earlier, and her husband Walter. After pleasantries were exchanged, Marilyn discussed when she could meet him to discuss the service order. She offered to stop by his office the next morning.

After the reception, he and his family walked home. Home—it actually seemed like *home*. And there was something else that he couldn't quite put his finger on that seemed different—something inside his soul.

CHAPTER 3
CHRISTOPHER DUNN

Christopher laughed when he saw the latest tabloid pronouncing his torrid affair with Liza. They're like a pack of wolves, he thought—sniffing for meat. Well, perhaps they were getting the scent that all was not well in the Dunn household. He and Julie were getting very close to ending their farce of a marriage. They had played it out now for almost six years. It should have ended before it began. Thoughts of Mary again burdened him with guilt—guilt and regret.

What a fool he had been to discard her. He closed his eyes and tried to remember her beautiful face. Where are you Mary? he wondered. He had tried to find her but she had vanished without a trace. Not even her closest friends knew why she had so abruptly left or where she had gone. He again admonished himself for never delving into her family history during their conversations. How could they have missed discussing that? All he remembered her saying was that she was raised on a farm in Michigan—and Michigan is a very large state.

He remembered their first meeting. She was the first person he saw when he arrived at that cast party that evening, and the *only* person he saw all evening, actually. They chatted about all sorts of things—the play, his music, her career. She teased him about his long hair, which he admitted he was delinquent in getting cut.

During the next few weeks he spent a lot of time at the theater, and also with Mary. They had a lot of fun. They either had *coffee before, pizza after*, or just sat around the piano with a group of others and sang the musical scores he was currently working on.

He didn't know exactly when it happened (probably at first sight) but he thought they might be falling in love. Suddenly reality came crashing down on him. He was engaged to be married to Julie in six short weeks. He realized he needed to back away from Mary—and he did try. But then there was that final night.

He looked in vain for Mary to appear at the party that was given for him the night before he returned to London. He couldn't take his eyes off the door hoping that at any moment she would enter. When she failed to make an appearance he knew that he would have to see her one more time—and that last meeting changed him forever.

When she opened the door to her apartment she looked so beautiful. She was wearing a chenille robe and she had just washed her hair. When he asked her why she didn't come to the party, she started to cry. He then took her in his arms and there was no turning back. Their fate was sealed.

He truly intended to call off his wedding when he returned to London but the instant he stepped off the plane he felt as though he entered a vortex he could not escape from. He was immediately entangled in prenuptial dinner parties, and other activities with Julie, her family, and his family as well. He knew they would be extremely hurt by what he was contemplating.

The longer he waited the harder it became—they were in the midst of elaborate preparations for the wedding and he truly did care for Julie. He had known Julie for a long time and they had a long-standing engagement. He suddenly knew he could not end it.

As the days swept by, he knew he needed to talk to Mary. He tried several times to phone her, but just as the connection was in progress, he hung up. He did not know how to tell her that he was marrying Julie. Finally, he wrote a heartfelt letter to her and posted it a few days before his wedding. When he returned from his honeymoon, he found the letter had been returned to him—*addressee unknown*.

Through the years he had become very successful and somehow he believed it was all due to Mary. Everything he wrote, he wrote for her, and it was good.

CHAPTER 4

JOHN'S OBSESSION

It was now eight months since his installation at St. Luke's. Things had worked out exceedingly well. The children eased into their new schools nicely and quickly made friends. He felt he was slowly healing. He'd never stop missing Elizabeth, but felt he could now *live with* missing her.

He found life in Taylor Creek very rewarding and felt that his ministry was back on track once more. He was, however, becoming a little troubled lately with a continuing fascination with Marilyn Maier. He was still being awed by her beauty and talent, and charmed by her warm personality. As an organist she was excellent, but he noticed, also, that he was becoming obsessed with observing her—how she dressed, how she wore her hair on a particular day, and—oh God yes—her body. If Elizabeth knew she would kill him. (Well, she probably did know.)

At a church social, earlier that year, yet another of her talents surfaced. She and her brothers, Gary and Eddie, offered the entertainment for that particular gathering. He'd heard that she once appeared in a Broadway show for a brief time but never realized until that evening how good she was. She sang a well known gospel spiritual. She sang the first verse a cappella and she had a sweet rich voice that touched his soul. Then on the second and third verses her brothers joined in and accompanied her—Gary on the guitar and Eddie on the piano. She offered it in a kind of "blues" style, straight from her heart. She finished on a beautiful high note that took his breath away. He couldn't believe such a person existed right here in tiny little Taylor Creek.

Once he had stopped by her house to drop off a service insert. She lived in a very old turn of the century farmhouse which she had quite nicely decorated. It was warm and bright and he was quite impressed with what she had done to the place. She was baking bread and offered him a slice—it was still fresh and warm right out of the oven—and she served it with homemade strawberry jam (yet another talent)! Once more he couldn't help observing her appearance. She was wearing a blue sweater—the color of her eyes.

Then she invited him to take a walk down to the creek—it was spring and the wildflowers were blooming. She wanted him to see how incredibly beautiful it was. He had the most powerful urge to put his arm around her as they were walking together down the steep incline to the creek. He wondered how he was going to be able to continue to work with Marilyn with these obsessive thoughts—and it got worse!

Once he happened upon her while she was rehearsing a prelude at the organ. She didn't see him behind her, but she was wearing a silk blouse, open at the neck, and as she leaned forward, what he had left only to his imagination was suddenly revealed. He had a dream about her that night—one that he did not care to share with anyone.

He felt that his thoughts were becoming unhealthy and obsessive. He knew he was sexually deprived, but was he also sexually depraved? He was almost twice her age at forty-five. If he needed a companion for the rest of his life, he would be wise, considering his position, to be concentrating on someone closer to his own age, but he had no desire to search out another woman at this time. Then *why* was he continuing to be so captivated by this young woman?

He asked himself if he should have another talk with his bishop about the matter. Perhaps he needed to consider another move. But his children would be disappointed, and, he thought, so would he.

CHAPTER 5
MARILYN'S AWAKENING

Marilyn found she was very impressed with John Westin. He was an inspiring speaker and many of his sermons gave her food for thought—things that she needed to hear and she felt quite spiritually fed.

Pastor Westin was a very distinguished looking man—slightly graying at the temples. He was a big man, tall and stalwart, but he had a gentle, kind manner, and also a tongue-in-cheek sense of humor. He was a delight at committee meetings with his wit and sense of good fun. She found she enjoyed being around him.

Something happened, however, in recent weeks to change her perception of him. It happened the beginning of June during Vacation Bible School. She had enrolled Christy for the two week summer program. When she came to pick her up one day, all the children were out on the lawn playing a game, but John was holding Christy in his arms. Apparently Christy had fallen and hurt herself and John had picked her up to console her. When she saw Christy in his arms she saw a picture of a father holding his daughter. It so unnerved her that she stood motionless for a few moments lost in thought. The realization hit her so bluntly—Christy should have a father—she should have a father like John Westin!

During the next few weeks, she often thought of that incident. She didn't want to rob Christy of a father, yet she had not met anyone she deemed worthy of that honor—except for John Westin. He was, she realized, aside from Christopher, exactly the kind of man she wished for.

A week or so later, as she was leaving the church after a brief practice session, she saw John out in his yard. He wasn't wearing his usual garb but had on jeans and a T-shirt. She was again shocked by her reaction to him. She began to realize he was very well-built, masculine, and *sexy*! She looked at him—really looked at him, and she felt as though she had just awakened. She then quickly looked away muttering to herself, "Now that would really start the congregation humming if I carried on with the minister!"

She had occasionally dated since Christy's birth. She knew that she needed to "get a life" without Christopher. She did require certain qualities in a man and so far no one had sparked an interest. And now, John Westin, for some strange reason, was "stirring her coals."

She felt she needed to get a grip on herself. She had already caused one scandal in this community and to now be having these feelings for a man twenty years her senior was absolutely ludicrous. But she continued to be aware of John in a different way from that point on.

CHAPTER 6

THE PICNIC

July was the month of the annual church picnic. Marilyn again volunteered to do the "Fish Pond." It was the little children's event. She always enjoyed it as she had participated in it when she was a child. By purchasing a ticket (all proceeds went to missions) the child could then "fish" for a prize. They would throw their line into the pond (in this case over a curtain in a booth) and they would hook a prize. It was the most popular event for the kids.

Prizes for the fish pond were donated by members of the congregation and she had to collect them, wrap them and label them for either boy or girl. She then searched for volunteers to work behind the curtain in the booth during the picnic. She, herself, took a one hour shift. It was a lot of fun.

It was during her shift that something happened that shook her calm world. She was waiting for the next "bite" when Pastor John ducked in to offer a last minute donation for the fish pond. He was just handing it to her when some women on the other side of the curtain began speaking. They were totally unaware that anyone was in the booth and overhearing them.

One woman was saying, "You know why Marilyn Maier is secretive about the father of her child?"

"No," the other woman responded, "why?"

"She was actually raped," she first woman eagerly related.

"Well that explains why she's always been so . . ." and the rest of the conversation was not understood.

Marilyn sat stonily silent. She could not understand how anyone could so callously have started such an ugly rumor.

Suddenly she felt John's hand on her shoulder—she had forgotten he was there. He then sat down beside her and all he did was look at her, and the kindness and concern he conveyed with his eyes meant far more than anything he could have said. And with his hand resting on her shoulder, she felt a strength emanating from him that strangely kept her from losing control. I need him here, she thought . . . oh, do I *need* him.

She somehow got through the rest of the day and after the picnic was over, it was decided that Christy go home with her grandmother.

"I'll just keep her for the night," her mother said. "She's so tired she'll be asleep before we get home."

Marilyn agreed that would be best as she had quite a bit more to do. She had to dismantle her booth and put it away in the picnic shed. She was also still a little shaken by the gossip incident earlier in the day and wondered how she could deal with the awful rumors and protect Christy from them as well. She was thankful Pastor John was there—he somehow helped her stay glued.

She at last got her booth taken down and put away and as she headed home, she thought it looked an awful lot like rain—they had finished up in the nick of time. When she got to her door, she realized she'd left her house keys in the picnic shed. Oh drat, she thought, I'll have to go back.

CHAPTER 7

THE STORM

After the picnic, John bid good-bye to Bethany and Michael as they were going on a trip with their grandparents (Elizabeth's mother and father). Elizabeth's parents had always spent a lot of time with the children. His own parents were deceased so these were the only grandparents his children knew and they were very close. They were going to the Mackinaw area and the children were eager to cross the bridge connecting the lower and upper peninsulas of Michigan. He was actually looking forward to a little time to himself to be alone with his thoughts.

The picnic had been a success except for the gossip incident involving Marilyn earlier that day. She was quite shaken. He wished he could have said or done something more for Marilyn this afternoon, but his instinct was to gather her up in his arms, and he knew he couldn't do that. She seemed calmed, though, when he put his hand on her shoulder.

John often wondered about Christy's father. He obviously had red hair, as Christy was a cute little redhead and no one in Marilyn's family had red hair. According to Mrs. Maier, who had once confided in him, Marilyn had always been very secretive about Christy's father. She never breathed a word about him except to say he was married. He seriously doubted the validity of the rape story.

He looked out the window and realized it was going to storm. He was glad that the weather held out for the picnic. As he looked toward the picnic shed behind the church he noticed that the side door of the shed was open. He thought it strange as he and a few others were the last to leave and he was certain they had closed everything but perhaps the wind had opened it. He decided to go look. The rain was coming down pretty heavy by the time he got into the shed—then he realized he was not alone.

Marilyn got back to the picnic shed as the rain was just beginning, and by the time she found her keys, John burst in. They quite startled one another.

"I left my house keys," she said, "I really didn't have my head on straight when I left here." Just then the rain was beginning to come down in torrents.

"I saw the door open and thought I'd better investigate . . . and I think we're going to be stuck in here for a while," John said, just as the thunder and lightning increased in their intensity.

"What about your children?" Marilyn exclaimed. "They're all by themselves in this."

"No, they're all right. They've left with their grandparents on a trip. They're probably driving out of this deluge by now."

"Oh, of course," Marilyn said, "I now remember Bethy talking about it . . . she was so excited."

The sky had darkened considerably and Marilyn then said, "My, it certainly is dark in here, isn't it? Do the lights work or is the breaker off?"

"I think the breaker is off," John began, and suddenly there was a tremendous bolt of lightning accompanied by a crash of thunder which obviously struck very close. Marilyn instantly lurched towards John and clung to him. She was trembling with fright. John instinctively held her close to him to calm her.

John continued to hold her and slowly realized he did not want to release her. It had been a very long time since he had held a woman and this woman was someone he'd wanted to gather up for a long time. Then he realized that she was holding on to him just as desperately. As the rain continued to batter down on the shed, they continued their embrace.

Finally Marilyn spoke. "Don't let me go . . ." She was totally spent with all of the emotional turmoil of the day and felt comforted in John's arms. She just wanted to linger there forever.

"I won't let you go," he said, knowing that somehow he needed to seize this moment—he had desperately yearned for a woman in his arms—this woman.

They continued their embrace for what seemed like a very long time. Then she lifted her face from his shoulder and her lips brushed his cheek—he then turned and kissed her. As their lips touched, John felt the lightning and thunder outdoors could not match what was happening inside the shed. They continued to kiss passionately, their emotions slowly getting out of control. Then, suddenly, John drew away, realizing he'd overstepped his boundaries. "Marilyn, I'm sorry, this is my fault . . . I am out of line, very much out of line . . ."

The rain outside had ebbed and it suddenly seemed very

quiet except for the sound of raindrops falling from the trees outside. Marilyn, too, was very quiet for a few moments, and then she said, somewhat to herself, "Why do the men I fall in love with always turn away from me?"

John couldn't at first comprehend her meaning. "What did you say?" he quietly asked.

Marilyn looked up at him then and whispered softly, "I guess I said I love you."

John was still holding her left hand. He slowly pulled her back in an embrace and whispered back, "I think I love you, too, Marilyn Maier." He kissed her then again, with tenderness and longing, his loneliness and desolation almost forgotten until reality again entered his consciousness.

"I think we need to talk," John finally said.

"Yes," replied Marilyn, "we've suddenly cut a new path, haven't we?"

They slowly parted, still holding hands.

"I've been harboring some very intense feelings for you, Marilyn, for quite some time."

"You have? Really? I thought it was just me having these sinful thoughts." she laughed.

"You've had sinful thoughts about me?" John exclaimed. "That's delicious! Seriously, though, Marilyn, I think we really need to analyze this . . . I'm much older than you . . ."

"No, John," Marilyn stopped him, "I don't want to hear this . . . please don't say it . . . I feel that I've finally found something so wonderful . . . I don't want it spoiled." She then put her arms around him, and they stood together embraced again in quiet wonder at their newfound bliss.

Finally, after a few moments, Marilyn said, "I really have to get home and call mom . . . see if Christy's okay. Will you give me half hour and then come to my place?"

John paused a moment and then said, "Yes, Marilyn, I'll come." They then walked hand in hand back through the wet field to Marilyn's car.

When John returned to the parsonage he quickly showered and put on some dry clothes. He managed to get a little damp from his run to the shed earlier. He was deep in thought about their encounter. What had happened? It caught them both by surprise, yet they both seemed totally in sync out there in the shed. There were so many negatives about this relationship. Marilyn needed someone younger—she probably hadn't thought things through. She was so young—she should have a man who could still have babies with her. He would have to make sure she understood what she was getting herself into. How he had loved holding her in his arms, though.

He drove the short distance to Marilyn's farmhouse and when he got to the front porch there was a note pinned to the screen door: *I'm probably in the shower—just come on in and have a glass of wine—it's on the dining room table.*

He walked in and found the wine as Marilyn had indicated. He poured himself a glass and sat down. The room was like a tranquilizer—what a wonderful place to come to after a storm. Time sort of stood still in this room, with all the furniture from a different era—very pleasant, he thought. Just then she emerged.

"It certainly feels good to get out of those grubby picnic clothes. I see you've changed also. You got pretty wet running to the shed, didn't you?"

"Yes, and probably just missed getting hit by lightning, too."

"Well, if it hadn't been for the lightning and thunder *things* might not have happened. Do you think God was getting us together," she laughed.

"Maybe . . . or maybe Elizabeth was trying to kill me," he said jokingly. "By the way, you took an awful chance pinning that note on the door . . . anyone could have walked in."

"True, but the only people that ever come here are my family . . . and you," and then she said with an amused expression, "I took a chance I'd be safe."

Marilyn then became serious, "John, you loved your wife very much. Do you feel as though you betrayed her today? I know you were joking, about her trying to kill you with the lightning and all, but you still miss her very much, don't you?"

"My life was almost totally destroyed when she died, and, yes, I still miss her . . . the kids miss her, but we've somehow managed to survive. Taylor Creek has helped us, the church, the people . . . and you've helped me, Marilyn. You know that now, don't you?"

"John, I've been thinking a lot since I came home . . . I feel we're stepping into dangerous territory here. Do you realize how the church could distort this? *Pastor cavorts with good girl gone bad* . . . that's how unmarried mothers are perceived in this community, you know? I could ruin your reputation . . . I realize that now. I don't want to cause problems for you . . . it seems as though I'm always causing problems for people."

"Believe me, Marilyn, you're not a problem for *me*! It's *you* I'm concerned about . . . and I've been doing a lot of soul searching as well. I'm far too old for you . . . you're still so young. Why would you want to get involved with me? You need to think about that, Marilyn. Have you?"

"Yes I have . . . more than you realize." Marilyn paused and also poured herself a glass of wine. "John, you've been in my thoughts so often lately. I told you tonight that I loved you. Did you know that I just then realized it? With all my heart, I knew it then."

All of John's reservations suddenly didn't seem important. He walked over to where Marilyn was standing and held her close. "I don't think I'll ever be able to let you go." He breathed the words softly into her hair.

He then made love to her and all the torments of his life were melted into oblivion.

CHAPTER 8
MARILYN & JOHN

In the weeks that followed, Marilyn and John spent a lot of time with one another. Marilyn was reluctant, however, to bring their relationship out into the open right away. She feared how it might affect John's standing in the church. John wanted to be forthright about it—he felt all the "sneaking around" might be more harmful if accidentally discovered by some members of the congregation.

Eventually they decided they would set the rumor mill in motion by having dinner together and being seen together in public places. It didn't take long, beginning with Marilyn's family, who questioned her at length about who she was "going out with" as she had asked her mother to sit with Christy several times. When she told her mother it was John Westin, she was surprised by her reaction.

"Oh, Marilyn," she exclaimed, "that's so wonderful. You know, I often saw you two standing next to one another and I would think to myself . . . *they make such a handsome couple . . . if only Marilyn could find a man like that* . . . and now you are a couple. I'm so happy. He's such a fine man."

"Mom, I thought you'd be put off by the age difference."

"Really? Oh I don't know . . . he seems *young* to me. Age is irrelevant, though, as long as you are happy."

Marilyn received the same reaction from her father and siblings. They were brimming over with enthusiasm, and Christy was wildly happy—she loved John.

John experienced a slightly different reaction from his family. Elizabeth's parents thought he had taken leave of his senses. They lived in a different state but had heard the news via telephone through Bethy and Michael.

"John, please think of the children," Elizabeth's mother

warned, "what can you be thinking, running about with a young unmarried mother?"

John hoped they would come around once they got to know Marilyn, but, of course, they were fiercely loyal to their daughter's memory and the idea of Marilyn usurping Elizabeth's role in his life was unthinkable to them. It would take time, he thought.

Bethany, on the other hand, was crazy about Marilyn. Even prior to their relationship, Bethany had always been bubbling over with *Marilyn did this* or *Marilyn did that*. She quite idolized Marilyn. Michael, though, was a different story. It was he who had expressed his doubts to his grandparents. He and his mother had been very close—he was not yet ready to allow anyone else to take her place. He might have problems with Michael.

The congregation, he thought, was about 80-20. He could judge people's reactions by their facial expressions. The ones that smiled "knowingly" and shook his hand a little longer were "for," and the one's that didn't quite look him in the eye and were coolly polite were "against." Not bad, thought John, there was bound to be some difference of opinion and it seemed that the majority was with them.

They announced their engagement at the Thanksgiving Day service. John thought it appropriate. He prepared a special sermon about it, reviewing all the things he was thankful for: He began with his congregation, for their love, concern and support of him since his arrival; the community and his beautiful surroundings; the love of his first wife, Elizabeth, and his beautiful children that were born out of that love; and finally, Marilyn, and how they had come to know one another and respect one another, and *need* one another and therefore would be marrying in the near future. After that, he felt that the opposition slowly began swaying toward the eighty percentile group.

They were married on New Year's Day. Bishop Carl Keen performed the ceremony and their witnesses were Bethy, Michael and Christy. Michael had come around some—due much to Marilyn who had a few conversations with him. He couldn't help but like Marilyn—she had done everything she could think of to allow him to accept her for herself—not as a new "mother," but as a friend. Michael was just beginning his teenage years and, of course, had a lot of other hormonal things going on as well. Elizabeth's parents, as well, were just a little more accepting of Marilyn.

After the wedding reception, which took place in the church fellowship hall, they left immediately for the Bahamas for their honeymoon. They basked in the warm sunshine which was a welcome change from the cold Michigan winter. Marilyn had brought two swimsuits and couldn't decide which one looked best on her. She tried on both trying to glean from John which he thought was the most becoming.

"Try on the other one again," John said.

So Marilyn changed back to the first. Then John said, "I'm not sure . . . try the second one on again," and suddenly Marilyn realized what he was doing when she saw the mischievous glint in his eye. Needless to say, they didn't make it to the beach for several hours.

They were very much in love and very happy. Marilyn's thoughts did not so often rest on Christopher anymore. He was there, in the background, Christy's biological father, but John was now "daddy" to Christy and soon he would be legally adopting her. They were a family—the five of them.

Marilyn had made a decision early with regard to Christopher. She decided she didn't want to tell John about him—she didn't want Christy's father *"hanging like a picture on our wall."* John argued that she knew about Elizabeth so why shouldn't he know about her first love. She somehow conveyed to John, without disclosing Christopher's great fame, that it would only be extra baggage in their marriage. Elizabeth was different, she said. She literally could not "haunt" them. She was now *gone*, and could not change things. Christy's father, on the other hand, could, and if John knew about him, he might find it difficult to be *comfortable*. What she couldn't tell him was that she wanted to spare him from the fear that their lives could suddenly appear on "Hard Copy."

Marilyn felt that maybe when Christy was older, she could disclose her father's identity to her, but that could wait. Now she felt secure in the knowledge that she was starting a new life and had a beautiful new family. Christopher was her past—John was her future.

CHAPTER 9
CONFLICT

John and Marilyn's lives seemed to flow easily through the next six years. They had decided early in their marriage that their family was "complete." Marilyn did not feel that John needed to pursue the surgery called a "vasovasostomy" so that he could reverse the vasectomy procedure that he had done while married to Elizabeth. She had Christy, and John had Michael and Bethany—together they had their "family." John worried that Marilyn would want another child, but Marilyn insisted that she was content with the way things were.

Michael had graduated from high school and had been accepted at Northwestern University and they were very proud of him. Christy adored both Bethany and Michael and looked upon them as her big brother and sister, and they, in turn, looked upon Christy as their own "kid sister." It seemed as though nothing could penetrate Marilyn's happiness—but it did!

It all began with a song. Marilyn heard it on the car radio as she was driving home from Hillsburg one day. It was a song from a new Christopher Dunn musical and it was called "Where Are You Now, Mary My Love," and it went on, *I have searched far and wide to the heavens above . . . Again and again I relive that sweet night . . . where may I find thee, my Mary, my life,* and each succeeding verse seemed to carry a message straight to Marilyn! She stopped her car at the side of the road—she was shaken. He couldn't be speaking to her through his music, could he? All of the old emotions and turmoil once again began to churn within her. She had heard through the media that he had divorced a few years ago, and since then the media had him coupled with many assorted stars and women of note. She tried not to focus her attention on that, but it had been difficult.

She and John had even once gone to one of his musicals,

together with some friends of theirs. John, of course, didn't realize the tremendous effort it took on her part to play the part of normalcy, both before and after (Christopher's music still had a powerful effect on her), but at least John could enjoy it normally and she somehow got through that evening. But now there was this new musical—this song. *It is just a coincidence . . . just a coincidence that the heroine's name is Mary*, she kept repeating to herself. *We haven't seen each other for years . . . he's forgotten all about me . . . it's just a coincidence*! She then regained her composure and continued driving home.

As was the case with all of the Christopher Dunn musicals, the song became very popular and was played often—on the radio, television—and even figure skaters performed to it. If his aim was to locate Marilyn, he was hitting his mark. But she still could not allow herself to believe the song was meant for her—she couldn't allow it!

About a month later, upon returning from a trip to Northwestern, after they had ensconced Michael in his dorm, another coincidence rocked Marilyn's world. They were at O'Hare Airport waiting to board their flight at an American gate when suddenly a couple of people she had worked with in *Night Train* appeared before her.

"Mary . . . Mary Mayer . . . yes it *is* you."

"Melanie, Bill . . . how nice to see you," Marilyn stammered.

"We sat there across the aisle looking at you for the longest time, wondering if we should approach you. Bill said it definitely was you . . . I wasn't sure." Melanie gushed. "Where in the world have you been? Talk about someone dropping out of existence. And this gorgeous hunk must be your significant other?" she went on, eyeing John.

"Yes," Marilyn replied, "this is my husband, John Westin." She then took John's arm. "John, these are two old friends of mine, Melanie Albert and Bill Frothe. We were in *Night Train* together . . . about a hundred years ago." Marilyn laughed.

"It has been a long time," Bill said. "Nice to meet you John . . . Westin? . . . was it?"

"Yes, John Westin," John replied. "Very pleased to meet you both."

"Gosh honey, it's been ages," Melanie said. "By the way, did Chris Dunn ever contact you Mary? He was avidly searching for you . . . when was that, Bill? About four or five years ago?"

"Actually he spoke to Vivian quite recently," Bill said. "We thought he might have created a wonderful part for you in one of his productions. Obviously you didn't take him up on it, Mary."

"No," Marilyn said, clutching John's arm, "he hasn't contacted me. However, I'm out of the business now. I'm a happily married lady and a minister's wife. The stage is far behind me."

"So Mary, you hitched up with a man of the cloth," Bill said. "You always were such a *good* girl," and then smiling at John, he continued, "she was a very *good* girl, John, I can vouch for her from when we knew her . . . I don't know about *now*, though," he added as a witticism.

John smiled, and said, "I'm still keeping her pretty much in line."

Melanie laughed and gave John a pat on the arm, then turning to Marilyn, she said, "Listen, Mary, you *should* call Christopher Dunn, though. I understand he's just about asked *everyone* if they've seen you. Just call him to get him off all of our backs, would you?"

"I'll do that," Marilyn said. They then exchanged some general information regarding their current situations. Marilyn reluctantly had to reveal where they lived in Michigan. Bill and Melanie also gave her their telephone numbers in New York. Just then Melanie and Bill heard their final boarding call being announced and they all said their hurried good-byes, with promises of keeping in touch in the future.

Marilyn couldn't describe the feeling of dread that overcame her after they had left. She felt as though she might faint. She looked at John. *John knew!* She could see it in his eyes. He was a very intelligent man and it wouldn't have taken much in what had just transpired for him to put two and two together.

"Now do you understand?" Marilyn asked.

"You were right, Marilyn," John said, " . . . he would have *hung like a picture on our wall!*"

Marilyn told John everything then—it all tumbled out. She told him about her fear of the media and how she wanted to protect their family. She told him how she was convinced that it was wise to keep that part of her life from him as she knew that Christopher would shadow their marriage because of his great fame.

John still seemed slightly stunned. "I knew you were in a Christopher Dunn musical," John said, "but I never imagined you knew him personally. I somehow still can't believe it . . . it's unbelievable that Christy's father is Christopher Dunn!"

"John, if Christopher does find me . . . please . . . he can't know about Christy. It is the only way I can think to protect her. Can you imagine what the tabloids would do with that information?"

"I agree, but are you going to call him as you said you would?"

"Of course not. I only hope that he won't contact me. Bill and Melanie may not remember where I told them we lived, should Christopher ask."

"Yes, they may not have retained that part," John agreed.

During the flight home, Marilyn rested her head on John's shoulder. She wondered what he was thinking. What his reaction was to the fact that Christopher wanted to see her! She wondered what he would think if he heard that song—he was bound to hear it, or probably had heard it. Maybe he hadn't made the connection yet. Oh, God, she thought, will I ever be free of this turmoil?

CHAPTER 10

CONFRONTATION

During the next few weeks John became increasingly disturbed by his new knowledge of Christy's parentage. He struggled with many emotions. How could this man have left Marilyn in such a predicament? She loved him very much once—that was obvious. Did she yet? And why was he trying to re-establish contact? What were Christopher Dunn's motives? He had to know.

As he struggled with all his unanswered questions, he also did a little investigation without Marilyn's knowledge. He had always been aware of this famous man, but had never paid any close attention to him until now. He bought some tapes of his music and checked out magazine articles about him from the local library. He was *something*—made the top ten most eligible men last year—he was number two! Every woman's *heartthrob*!

Marilyn was right to have kept the truth from him. He felt consumed with jealousy. He always viewed Christy's father as "some man," and he could have dealt with "some man," or any man now, but he couldn't seem to deal with Christopher Dunn.

He prayed about it constantly, asking for some insight in handling his emotions. He finally came to the conclusion that he needed to confront Christopher Dunn face to face. His father had once offered him a valuable lesson years ago—*identify your fears, face them, then you can live with them.* John had identified his fear, and now he had to "face" his fear—the fear of Christopher Dunn!

He also decided to do this without Marilyn's knowledge. He disliked the fact that he was being deceptive but he thought it would be best for Marilyn if he did not tell her. He in no way intended to "drop the ball" as far as Christy was concerned, but he wanted to express to Dunn that Marilyn and he were building a life together and he needed to find out why he was so intent on getting in touch with her, and also, the meaning behind the song, "Where Are You Now, Mary, My Love"—as if he didn't already know!

John was scheduled to go to a pastor's conference in November. He thought it might be a good opportunity to try to get in touch with Dunn, since the conference was near New York. Apparently Dunn had an apartment in New York where he occasionally lived. He looked through Marilyn's date book and found Melanie Albert's phone number that she had so hastily written down that day in the airport. He copied Melanie's number down to take along with him to his conference. He would have to ask her assistance in getting in touch with Christopher Dunn—he wasn't exactly listed in the phone book!

The afternoon that he arrived at the hotel for the conference, he made the call. He was told by Melanie that she would have to get in touch with a friend, Christopher Dunn's secretary, and have her relay the message. He gave her his telephone number at the hotel and waited.

John had made his call at 2:30 in the afternoon—he received a call from Christopher Dunn's secretary at 6:30. Her name was Jennifer Willis, she said, and she was calling to inquire as to the nature of John's business with Mr. Dunn. John said that what he needed to discuss was of a personal nature, and it was regarding his wife, whom Christopher had known as Mary Mayer. Jennifer asked him to hold.

In a few minutes she returned to the phone and said that Christopher Dunn wanted to see him and asked if John could meet him at (she gave him an address) at about 11 a.m. the next day.

"I'll be there," John said. He knew he'd have to skip the first day of the conference. The following morning he was at the address that was given to him.

After being ushered through some security, Jennifer Willis, herself, escorted John to a posh penthouse suite in view of Central Park in New York City.

Christopher was standing at the window when he walked into the room. He turned when he heard John, and for a few moments they just stood, observing one another. Christopher spoke first.

"You're not going to shoot me, are you, Reverend Westin?"

"No . . . I'm not going to shoot you, Mr. Dunn," John replied.

"Good. Call me Christopher, by the way." He walked closer to John.

"All right, Christopher . . . then you may call me John." They were both still standing and the room was static with tension.

"John, I'm sorry, please sit down." He then motioned John to a chair by the window as he chose one directly opposite.

He was quite good looking, John thought, reddish hair, British accent, and he saw Christy's features in him. There was no doubt that he had fathered her.

John began, "I would like to ask that you keep our meeting in confidence, at least for the time being. Marilyn doesn't know I'm here . . ."

"Marilyn?" Christopher interrupted.

"Yes, Marilyn is her real name . . . Mary Mayer was a stage name she adopted."

"That explains why I couldn't find her," Christopher said. "I called Melanie last night. She told me that you wanted our meeting to remain discreet. She was so certain that Mary would call me after they spoke at the airport that it never occurred to her to tell me that she'd seen her . . . anyway, you must know that I always supposed that Mary had married someone, had a bunch of kids . . . do you have children?"

"Yes," John held his breath, "we have a family" and left it at that. Then John continued, "The reason I asked to see you is that I've been brooding about a couple of things. May I get right to the point?"

"Please . . ." Christopher exhaled.

"After my first wife, Elizabeth, died, I was filled with a tortured emptiness. My life, as I knew it, seemed changed forever. But I made it through the darkness, with the help of God, and into the light. Marilyn was that light for me. I love her very much and I don't want to lose her. And so, Mr. Dunn . . . Christopher . . . the song, "Where Are You Now, Mary My Love" . . .'worries' me . . . and I also need to know the reason you want to contact my wife?"

Christopher then spoke thoughtfully and slowly. "When my lyricist and I worked on that song, I told him that it would either bring me Mary or an irate husband. Unfortunately, the latter applied. But actually, I did use the song as an opportunity to ferret out Mary. It adapted well for this musical as well. You see, I have tried in every way possible to find Mary . . . Is Mary . . . Marilyn happy?"

"Yes," John said, "our life together is wonderful . . . that is . . . until we ran into Melanie and Bill at the airport that day, and now we both feel a little threatened about your desire to get in touch with her, and, of course, that song!"

Christopher continued, "As I told you, I have been trying to find Mary for a long time. You see, I wrote Mary a letter before I married Julie. She never received that letter . . . it was returned to me. Apparently Mary had moved and left no forwarding address. I still have the letter, John. I just want her to have it . . . It's somehow very important to me. Do you understand?"

Not waiting for an answer he went on, "You know it's one thing being a *cad*, but I would like her to know I'm somewhat of a *decent cad*. I wouldn't have just ignored her like that without a word. It's been one awful burden on my conscience all these years . . . that's why I wrote the song and wanted to speak to your wife."

Christopher continued, "I won't deny that I hoped Mary would be desperately unhappy and still want me, but I also hoped she would *be* happy as well. John . . . I can see how she would be very happy with you . . . I'm glad she's married to someone like you."

As Christopher spoke, John felt all his fears slowly ebb away. His father was a wise man, he thought. He was thankful he had made the decision to speak to Dunn, to face that nameless fear. He found himself relax for the first time in weeks.

John then asked, "Would you like me to give Marilyn the letter? I would be most happy to."

"It would mean a lot to me if you would."

Christopher then walked into another room to retrieve it. As he returned, he said, "I've been carrying this around for a long time," and then handed it to John. "Just tell her, I'm sorry . . . she meant a lot to me . . . please. I didn't mean to interfere in your lives." He then looked John squarely in the eye and said, "Would you also please tell her one more thing? . . . Please tell her that I . . . made a mistake . . . I would like her to know that."

"Yes," John said, "I will tell her that."

"You are a very fortunate man," Christopher said. They then shook hands, both of them having gained a new respect for one another and both now having a lighter burden to bear.

John then returned to his conference.

Two days later, when John settled himself on the plane for his trip home, he knew he would have to confess to Marilyn what he had done. She would understand. He would give her Christopher's letter and hoped they could finally put her past behind them. He knew that Christopher would not interfere in their lives again. He could understand him somewhat better now. He liked and respected the man for his integrity, but also pitied him—all that wealth and fame had not brought him happiness. He hoped that he could someday find what it was he so yearned for.

It was about twenty minutes into the flight. John was reviewing his conference notes when suddenly the plane took a sudden plunge. Everything flew about the cabin. Oxygen masks suddenly were flung down from above . . . there was a lot of smoke . . . screaming . . . unspeakable terror—then—

darkness . . .

darkness . . .

darkness . . .
and suddenly John once again emerged from the darkness into the light. Elizabeth was there waiting for him—in the *light*.

CHAPTER 11

THE AGONY

Marilyn rushed to the gate to meet John's flight. She had just arrived and heard the announcement that the flight had been delayed. Lucky, she thought, as she was certain she was going to be late.

She couldn't wait to see John. He had been somewhat remote and distant in recent weeks and she knew they needed to discuss that. She guessed it was, in part, due to his finding out about Christopher and the fact that Christopher was attempting to contact her. They would have to work things out. She loved John fiercely and knew that they would somehow weather this together.

As she continued to wait, she noted that there were a lot of people surrounding the desk at the gate and there seemed to be a lot of confusion and discussion. She was just about to come forward and ask as to the reason for the delay and how much longer it would be, when someone announced, "Would all parties who are waiting for flight 428 from Newark please report to the desk." A slight tremor of apprehension descended upon her. She forced herself to be calm and walked up with a group of others.

"Flight 428 has experienced a problem," a woman behind the counter said. "Would all of you follow that gentleman (someone lifted his arm indicated it was he) to another waiting area and you will be kept informed as rapidly as we receive further information. Thank you."

Marilyn's apprehension suddenly grew more intense. She somehow followed the others, seemingly in slow motion. A feeling of panic struck her. She was being overwhelmed by the terror that suddenly filled her being.

When they arrived at the designated room, everyone began asking questions, all at once. "What was wrong? What had happened? Why were they delayed?" After what seemed like a very long time a group of people came in along with more uniformed airport personnel. They were told, then, that Flight 428 had crashed in Pennsylvania—they did not yet know all the details, but it seemed there were no survivors.

Marilyn felt dizzy—she was nauseous. Pandemonium followed. Someone spoke to her—took her hand, trying to do what they could to help. A feeling of horror swept over her—she thought she would lose her mind. Her whole life—her John—"Oh God—oh God—no—nooooo," she wailed. The initial shock gave way to an unspeakable agony.

The hours that followed were bewildering. Marilyn could not think rationally. Somehow they contacted Eddie and he, Joan and Gary came. They held her and they all cried together. Suddenly Marilyn felt a sense of duty for John's children. They needed to get Mike home. Gary said he'd call him.

The hours and days following the tragedy Marilyn felt suspended in space. Somehow they planned the funeral service. Throughout, there were so many visitors, phone calls, so many voices and faces and tears. Michael, Bethany, Christy and Marilyn clung to one another at the cemetery.

In the weeks that followed, she felt she had descended into some horrible nightmare she could never awaken from. Michael, Bethany and Christy stayed by her side. Somewhere in the middle of it all, a box was delivered from the airline. It contained "personal effects," they said, of the deceased. She at once became angry. "How can there be *effects*," she screamed. "What about John—what about his *effects*?" Michael quickly had the box put into the garage and it remained there.

Marilyn fell into depression and fatigue. It was difficult for her to sleep. She found pleasure in nothing. She was beginning to understand what John must have endured when Elizabeth died.

Christmas came and it was joyless. Her only comfort was in the children—they made the best of it, but they, too, were suffering. And then, New Year's Day, their wedding anniversary. Marilyn stayed in seclusion.

Sometime early in January the inevitable time came when she had to move out of the parsonage. A new minister and his family would soon be moving in. Her father still owned the Liebermann property and she expressed a desire to move back into the old farmhouse.

Marilyn found it almost the way she had left it, but some of the paint needed freshening up and she would have to fix up the guest room for Bethy. Bethy was invited to live with her grandparents, but she preferred to stay with Marilyn and finish high school in Hillsburg with her friends. Also, during the years that she lived with Marilyn, she had come to think of her as her "mother."

The entire congregation helped with the move and it was done in short order. Many boxes remained stored and she only unpacked what was absolutely necessary. She resumed her job at the hospital part-time—she needed to occupy herself and stay busy.

Slowly Marilyn's life began to regain a small regimen of normalcy—and then it was spring and Michael came home from school for spring break. Michael was beginning to look more and more like his father—he had the same build and facial features. They all took long walks through the woods together and then they would sit down by the creek and talk about John, their dad, remembering everything they could.

Michael reminded Marilyn that they still needed to go through his father's personal belongings. Marilyn thought it might be time—she had put it off too long. They decided to do it all together, as a family. John's things had been packed away in boxes during the move. Marilyn could not bring herself to deal with any of it at that time.

Most of it was stored in the basement and Michael began lugging the boxes upstairs to the living room, where they sat down and examined what they wanted to keep and what they wanted to donate to charity.

The last box Michael retrieved was the box the airline had sent. Marilyn had forgotten about it. Suddenly she didn't have the "stomach" to continue.

"You look through it, Michael," she said. She noticed that it contained a badly battered piece of luggage, partially ripped but still owning some contents. She saw a shirt she remembered packing before he left. Her eyes were again filling up with tears. She looked away.

Michael, Bethany, and Christy carefully sorted through the bag. They found some papers and notes they thought Marilyn should go through. They found his tape recorder—*how could his tape recorder survive and not he*? Marilyn wondered.

"Here's some kind of letter," Bethy said. "It's addressed to a Mary Mayer . . . who's she?" and then she threw it down with the other papers.

Marilyn at first thought she must have misunderstood Bethy. "May I see that?" she asked.

"Sure . . . do you know who that is?" Bethy asked.

Marilyn didn't reply but stared down at the envelope in her hands. She was dumbfounded. She saw that it was addressed to her New York apartment. The return address said DUNN! Oh my God, she thought. She looked at the postmark—the date was about the time she returned to Michigan thirteen years ago! However, did this get into John's luggage? Her face must have looked ashen.

"Marilyn, are you okay?" Michael asked.

"Mom, what's wrong? You look so funny," Christy said alarmingly. "Mom?"

Bethany came over to her and said, "I'm sorry, I didn't know that letter was going to affect you so badly. I shouldn't have given it to you."

"I'm okay Bethy . . . please just excuse me for a while . . . I think I need to lie down. Don't worry, I'm all right."

Marilyn took the letter and walked into her bedroom and shut the door. She sat on her bed, trying to understand how in the name of God this letter happened to be in John's possession.

CHAPTER 12
THE LETTER

In the privacy of her bedroom Marilyn examined the letter closely. It had been stamped *addressee unknown*. This letter had been returned to London! How could it possibly have been in John's belongings? She kept asking herself this question over and over again. She then looked to see if it had been opened—it had not. She reached for the letter opener (her hands were shaking), and gently opened the letter.

Dear Mary,
   By the time you read this letter I will be married to Julie. It was not a decision that I came by easily. Is it possible to love two women? My answer to that is "yes."
   Mary, I want you to know, I will never forget you. They say everyone has a soul mate. Was that what it was with us? We were drawn to one another immediately. I will remember so many moments that we shared.
   I'll remember the times we went out with the cast, you and I. Being the only "singles" in the group, we quite often ended up being "paired," and I rather liked that.
   I'll miss hearing you sing my songs as I am writing them. Your voice always made the music sound so much better to my ear.
   I'll miss looking into your beautiful eyes, and seeing your generous warm smile.
   I'll never forget the time we went to that amusement park and rode on the Ferris wheel. I never knew anyone that was so terrified of heights. Remember when I reminded you that we had a pretty good chance of surviving until the ride was over, and you gripped the edge of the seat so tightly it made me laugh? And then I put my arms around you—I just wanted to keep my arms

around you then, Mary. That's why I suggested we take another ride, and then you gave me that "are you mad?" look.

I'll miss your laughter. Especially when we pulled that practical joke on Norman. You had tears running down your face. Remember his expression when he pulled out all that stuffing? Night Train *was never the same!*

We laughed, we sang, we loved—for a very short time, Mary. Much too short.

The night before I left we expressed our love to the highest degree. I want to hold on to that Mary. It was very precious to me.

When I came back to London, Julie was waiting for me with love and trust shining out of her eyes. Julie and I have a long history, Mary—much longer than ours. I couldn't bring myself to end either relationship, yet I knew whichever one I chose, I would be causing great pain to one of you, and to myself as well.

I am writing to you, Mary, as my pen seems to convey my feelings best—whether it be with words or music.

Remember me once in a while, Mary. You will find happiness with another, of that I am certain. I will always be jealous of that lucky one . . . whoever he might be.

Forever my love,

Christopher

Marilyn's eyes welled with tears. Now, after all these years, she finally understood. He loved her enough to write this letter—this letter—*where, how, why* did John have this letter?

After reading the letter once more she put it in her bureau drawer. She didn't have the energy to "wonder" about it any further.

Marilyn's *bureau drawer* began to be her main focus of attention after that. Her eyes were constantly drawn to it—and then the entire bureau seemed to "light up" when she entered the room. She couldn't put its contents out of her mind. She would wake up in the middle of the night and stare at her bureau drawer! When she couldn't bear it any longer, she decided to call Christopher.

Marilyn called Melanie Albert to ask for Christopher's private phone number.

"Hi Honey," she said. "It's so good to hear from you. How is that handsome husband of yours?"

Marilyn paused and then quietly said, "John was killed, Melanie, in a plane crash last November."

"Oh my God, Mary . . . I'm so very sorry," Melanie said. "What an awful thing to have happened. Oh honey . . . are you okay?"

"I'm doing better now, but it was the most awful thing I have ever had to endure, but thank you for your concern. Anyway, Mel, could you possibly give me Christopher's private number? I have a question to ask him."

"Sure honey . . . then you knew about your husband's call then?"

Marilyn stopped short. "What did you say? . . . My husband's call?"

Melanie was quiet for a moment and then reluctantly said, "Yes . . . well, he asked me not to tell you, but I supposed . . . you . . . I thought it was some kind of a surprise for you."

Marilyn began to understand the mystery . . . John called Christopher. Now she had to learn what had transpired.

"Mel, I just need to clear something up with Christopher. It's about that call."

"Well, he did more than call, honey," Melanie said, "they had a meeting too. Chris called me and said he was meeting your husband the next day and asked if I knew anything about him. I told him we'd met briefly at the airport and he was a real nice guy . . . a minister. By the way, Mary, why did you never call Chris . . . you said you would?"

"Well . . . there were reasons Mel . . . one of which was that I didn't have his phone number."

"Oh sure honey . . . I *really* am sorry about your husband . . . let's see now. I know I have Christopher's number here somewhere . . . oh here it is . . ."

Marilyn copied down the number Melanie gave her. She copied it down on the back of the envelope of Christopher's letter.

Marilyn needed to collect her thoughts before she called Christopher. Now everything was making sense. Obviously John, always a person who wanted to understand his problems, went right to the source. Dear, dear John. Perhaps she didn't need to call Christopher after all. John had accomplished what he wanted. He would have given her the letter and explained everything and they then would have carried on with their lives as before. The thought suddenly sobered her. She missed him so desperately.

Marilyn didn't call Christopher—he called her—two days later! It was a Sunday afternoon and Marilyn had just returned from a church luncheon when the phone rang.

"Mary, this is Christopher."

Marilyn suddenly felt as though she were out of her body, she couldn't find her voice. She had not spoken to him for so many years.

"Hello Christopher," she weakly said.

"Mary, I spoke with Melanie yesterday. She told me. I'm very sorry."

Marilyn couldn't say anything.

"Mary, perhaps I shouldn't have called. I need to know, though, when did this happen? Did your husband give anything to . . ."

Marilyn interrupted him. "I have the letter . . . it was in his personal . . . it was in his baggage. The airline returned it to me."

"My God . . . it happened right after we talked then?"

"Yes," Marilyn said.

No one spoke for a few moments. Finally Christopher said, "I asked him to give you a message, Mary . . . I asked him to tell you that . . . I made a mistake."

(Silence)

"I told him he was a fortunate man," Christopher added.

(Silence)

"We parted shaking hands, I quite liked him," Christopher further added.

Marilyn began sobbing, she could not control her emotions.

"Mary? Please Mary don't . . . I'm sorry . . . (long pause) . . . might I see you?"

"No, Christopher," Marilyn sobbed, "no . . . no . . . I can't see you . . . not yet anyway. I can't . . . I'm sorry."

"Mary?" Christopher asked, "please let me know when I can . . . I will wait . . . as long as it takes . . . I will wait. All right?"

"All right . . . I'm sorry . . . I can't stop crying . . . Goodbye Christopher."

"I've never stopped loving you, Mary." (long pause) Christopher then hung up.

Marilyn held the receiver to her ear long after Christopher's call, trying to sort out all of her emotions.

CHAPTER 13
CHRISTY

Christy hid her makeup in the side compartment of her book bag. Her mom disapproved, but she wanted to wear it tonight at the football game. Robin said the eyeshadow and lipstick made her look sixteen and "beautiful." Christy didn't know why her mom wouldn't at least let her wear a little lipstick—after all she was thirteen. Besides that, she was tall for her age. Her mother said she had also been tall at age thirteen but then stopped growing. Christy hoped she would stop growing, too, she didn't want to be a "giant," but it was fun passing for sixteen now.

Tonight was the Hillsburg High School homecoming game and she and Robin were going together. They would sit in the bleachers, as far away from her mom, Uncle Ed and Aunt Joan as possible. She didn't want her mom to notice the makeup. Bethy was homecoming queen and it was a "big deal" tonight. Christy was proud of Bethy—she was very popular. Bethy was a senior this year and would be going to college next year—probably to Northwestern as Michael did. She would miss her. Then it would be just her and mom again.

She could barely remember when it had been just the two of them. She remembered when her mom and dad got married, though. That was when she was six. Now her dad was dead—well not her real dad—but he seemed like a real dad to her. That was a year ago when he died in that awful plane crash. She really missed him. He always said that Bethy was his "*little girl*" and she was his "*little, little girl.*" She'd better stop thinking about him or she'd start crying again.

She looked in the mirror and saw her face without makeup. Yuk—I look like a young kid, she thought. She examined her features, her green-gray eyes, the small sprinkle of freckles, her long red hair. I wonder if I look like my real dad, she thought.

Once she asked her mom about him. All she said was that he was a really fine man but that he was married to another lady. God gave her John to take his place as her daddy, and she didn't say anything else. Christy knew that she probably shouldn't ask any more questions. Mom got that look where you knew when to stop.

She probably would see Timothy tonight. He was a sophomore and really "cute." She had to look her best for him! Maybe she could wear her mom's green wool scarf—it was really chic and the color worked well on her. She didn't think her mom would mind if she borrowed it. Her mother had left for work earlier than usual this morning so she'd have to try to find it by herself. She still had time, the bus wasn't coming for another twenty minutes.

She thought maybe her mom kept the scarf in her bureau drawer. She began to search for it, trying to be careful not to disturb anything. She finally found it way at the bottom. In pulling it out, tough, she got hold of some kind of letter. She started to put it back when something about it looked familiar to her. When she saw the name on the envelope, Mary Mayer, she suddenly remembered. That was the day they went through those boxes and mom got all funny when she saw this letter. Christy wondered why she kept it. She started to put it back, but curiosity got the better of her. Guiltily, she removed the contents and read them.

Christy often remembered, later in life, the morning of this momentous revelation. She was convinced that it was intuition that guided her to the appropriate conclusions. She was very young but had somehow figured it out.

As she read the letter, one thing leapt out at her. This Mary Mayer didn't like Ferris wheels. Funny, she thought, her mom didn't like Ferris wheels, either. She hated them. She always said, "I'm okay with heights as long as I have walls around me . . . but just a little bucket? . . . uh, uh!"

As she sat there pondering the letter, she had an overwhelming thought. Could this be a letter from her real dad? Why would her mother hide it? Sometimes people would call mom, Mary, just as a nickname, and mom did say her real dad married someone else, just as this man in the letter had done.

Then she noticed his name was Christopher . . . her name was Christy! No last name? She looked at the envelope again. Dunn with a London address. Dunn? Christopher Dunn? Christy's heart was pounding. She couldn't think. Oh Geeze, she would miss her bus! She hastily put the letter in its place and raced to the bus stop. She was in a trance most of the way to school and Robin thought she was sick.

Christy knew who Christopher Dunn was—everybody knew who Christopher Dunn was. Christy had seen his picture on the cover of *People* many times—HE HAD RED HAIR!!! Between periods, she asked Nicole if she had any magazines in her locker with a picture of Christopher Dunn in them. She found one and gave it to her. Christy went into the girls room and gazed at it. Then she looked in the mirror—she looked like him—SHE DID!! She could barely contain her excitement at her newfound knowledge.

Robin's mom took them out for burgers after school and then dropped them both off at the football field. They slunk up into the bleachers, well out of sight from where her mom, Uncle Ed and Aunt Joan were seated. They quickly applied their lipstick and eyeshadow. Christy couldn't contain herself any longer.

"Robin, I think I know who my real dad is!" She exclaimed.

"Who?" Robin asked.

"I think he's Christopher Dunn." Christy said.

"Oh, sure . . . and the Pope's not Catholic." Robin said disgustingly.

"No, Robin . . . I found a letter from him this morning in my mom's drawer . . . REALLY!"

"You're kidding."

"NO I'M NOT! I'll show it to you sometime."

Then, a week later, the opportunity presented itself and Christy showed Robin the letter. They were giddy with excitement. Christy swore Robin to secrecy. She feared her mom would not approve of what she had done.

Christy began to wonder how to handle this newfound knowledge. She desperately wanted to know if her hunch was right but could not bring herself to ask her mom about it. She felt guilty and somehow knew her mom would not be pleased with her. At every opportunity she took the letter out and examined it. She had noticed numbers on the back of the envelope, written in pencil, and she and Robin wondered about them. One day Robin suggested that they might be a telephone number. Maybe, thought Christy.

Then one day Christy had to stay home from school due to a cold and sore throat. Her mom told her to stay in bed, drink lots of fluids, and that Gran would stop by to check on her throughout the day. She said she would call several times, also, to make sure she was all right.

Christy was bored. She once again thought about the letter and wrestled with the thought of trying to "dial" that number that was on the back of the envelope. She finally gathered up her courage and dialed. She got a recording—"*Hi, this is Chris. Leave your number, I'll ring you back*"—and that was it. Christy hung up the phone as though it were a viper. Oh geeze—mom will see that on her phone bill, she worried. After that, she vowed she would never again attempt to call.

But the voice on the answering machine haunted Christy—it haunted her so much that she told Robin she would have to call the number again, just to hear the voice—and she did. She did it right before classes from a pay phone at school, right after the Thanksgiving break.

CHAPTER 14

BREAKTHROUGH

Christy didn't know it, but Christopher had just returned from London and was entering his apartment as the phone was ringing. He still had his travel bag slung on his shoulder and threw his keys on the table in order to catch the phone. He was expecting a call and wanted to pick it up before his machine took it.

"Hello," he said . . . no one responded.

He was just about to hang up when he heard a very young, tenuous voice say, "Is this Christopher Dunn?"

Once more he almost put the receiver back, thinking he'd have to get his private number changed once more. Something stopped him, however, and he thought he might at least try to find out who this was. "Who's calling, please?"

After a few seconds, the young voice continued, "My name is Christy Westin. Are you Christopher Dunn?"

Christopher heard the name, Westin, which made him take pause. "Yes . . . I'm Christopher Dunn. Why are you calling?"

"Do you know my mom, Marilyn Westin?" she asked.

"Yes, I do," he answered.

"I think you might be my real dad," she said.

Christopher felt as though an explosion had just occurred. He just stood there and held the phone, trying to think . . . this must be some prank, some sick joke.

Then the girl said, "I shouldn't have called you . . . my mom will be so angry with me. Please don't tell her . . . I just wanted to hear your voice on the answering machine, that's all . . ." Just then a recording interrupted and asked for more coins. The call was disconnected.

Christopher stood a moment as though in a stupor. She sounded genuine—no one could fake that tremulous voice. He paced around the room trying to make sense out of this, his thoughts in turmoil. She said her name was Christy . . . Westin. Why would she believe he was her *father*?

Christopher still had his jacket on and his bag was within reach. He snatched up the bag, left his apartment, haled a cab and asked to be driven to the airport. He found his cellular phone and contacted his private jet service. He discussed his destination with the pilot and they assured him they could get him "close" but that he would probably have to rent a car to get him the rest of the way.

Ever since he had called Mary early last summer he had hoped she would call him. He said he would wait for her. He wanted to give her time—enough time. He feared if he didn't, she might refuse to see him again, but now he was through waiting.

After his plane landed he donned his usual disguise which consisted of a baseball cap worn backwards and dark glasses. His pilot discreetly rented an automobile for him and he was given a map of the area. He knew Mary lived in Taylor Creek but he didn't know her exact address. He checked the local phone book when he got to Hillsburg and found her address listed as 901 Liebermann Road.

Hillsburg was about ten miles away from Taylor Creek, but he couldn't find Liebermann Road on the map! It was beginning to snow—big, soft, fluffy flakes. He thought he'd better stop at a filling station and ask for directions. As luck would have it, the filling station attendant lived on Taylor Creek Road, and he told him exactly how to find Liebermann Road.

"It's a dead-end road . . ." he said, "only house on it is the Liebermann house. Just go four miles down Taylor Creek Road and watch for the windy curve . . . you'll see Liebermann Road right there . . . it only goes right. Can't miss it." Then he looked at Christopher rather strangely. "You need those dark glasses on a cloudy day like this?"

"Snow blindness," Christopher said quickly. He thanked him, and grinning, returned to his automobile.

It began snowing quite heavily—the hills and valleys were blanketed with a white veil—every tree branch was covered with a soft layer of snow. It seemed to be whispering down to earth in a quiet hush. The song "Where Are You Now, Mary My Love," played in his mind and he marveled at the fact that she had existed here, all these years, in this remote part of the world amidst this beautiful landscape.

He saw the place where the filling station attendant had said to watch for Liebermann Road, and as he had said, it lay beyond the curves. He turned and started down a very narrow, gravel road. When he had traveled about a quarter of a mile he saw a gate, obviously where the road ended. Just before the gate, to the right, he saw the farmhouse. It was a white farmhouse with a curl of smoke rising from its chimney. It had a clothesline outside with a bird feeder hanging from it. It had a wide, grand, front porch with wicker furniture, and by the railing there were pumpkins, left over from Thanksgiving, no doubt.

He parked his car and walked up to the front door and knocked. Mary opened the door. She had a look of disbelief on her face. He just looked at her. He drank her in, like a man who had thirsted too long. She was even more beautiful than he remembered. The years had enhanced her beauty, lending her maturity and grace. She wore a blue plaid flannel shirt and jeans, and her hair was shorter than he remembered it, but just as beautiful—just gently touching her shoulders.

She looked at him for a long while also and then said, "Christopher . . . come in . . . out of the cold."

He walked in and saw there was a wood fire crackling in the fireplace and he also caught the aroma of something baking.

She said, "You are just about the last person on earth I expected to see standing outside my door." Just then a buzzer sounded from the other room. "I'm sorry," she said, " . . . that's my bread . . . I have to take it out of the oven . . . excuse me for just a second."

He took off his jacket and laid it on a chair by the piano. He noticed a picture of a girl on the piano . . . a young girl with red hair. As he looked at her, he fleetingly saw himself in her face . . . and then he *knew* . . . this must be Christy. He then walked into the kitchen . . . a warm inviting place. He saw the view of a winding creek from the window by the sink. She saw that he had followed her and smiled. "This will just take a second," she said.

"That really smells delicious," he said, realizing those were the first words he'd uttered upon entering the house.

"I like to make my own bread . . . just like my mama taught me," she said.

As she was placing the bread on racks to cool, he said to her, "Tell me about Christy."

She was taken aback. He knew he had struck a chord. After a moment's hesitation she said, "Why would you ask me about . . ."

Christopher stopped her, "Just tell me about Christy, Mary."

"But why are you . . ."

"TELL ME, MARY," Christopher again implored.

She paused a moment, and then, taking a deep breath, "I tried to tell you once, but you were on your honeymoon."

Christopher then walked over to her and cupped her face in his hands and looked deeply into her eyes. Her eyes were welling with tears . . . he kissed her eyes, tasting their saltiness . . . he kissed her forehead . . . he kissed her mouth . . . and then he put his arms around her and held her near to him . . . and his song continued to play in his mind . . . *Here I have found thee, my Mary, my Life* . . .

They didn't see their daughter Christy, smiling at them through the kitchen window.

CHAPTER 15
FULL CIRCLE

    Christy got a ride home from school with Robin's mom. She was grateful, as it was a little faster than taking the bus. She had a dreadful day. How could she have done such a foolish thing? She just wanted to get home and confess everything to her mom and beg forgiveness.
    When she walked up her driveway she noticed a car that she didn't recognize. As she walked along the porch to the door, she ducked to look in the kitchen window. Then she saw Christopher Dunn—holding her mom. She smiled and knew her mom wasn't going to be upset with her after all. Her *real dad* had finally come home.
    She turned and walked to the edge of the porch—then looking up at the snowflakes drifting down towards her she said, "Daddy John . . . thanks for helping me out," and then she blew him a kiss.

The End

About the Author

Ms. Nottingham very much enjoyed writing this, her "first novel," and is currently working on a second one. After retiring, she found she truly needed to occupy her mind and express her creativity in some fashion.

The author divides her time equally between Southwest Michigan and Central Florida, and takes delight in antiquing, music, and thoroughly spoiling her three *remarkable* grandchildren.